Downwind from Pemaquid

Sarah Jane Woolf-Wade

Cover illustration by Thomas Block
All page illustrations by the author, except for page 9, *Early Fishing Station,* mural by Claudia Coleman, used by permission of Colonial Pemaquid Museum, Pemaquid State Historic Site and page 29, *Tabby at the Tiller* by Consuelo Eames Hanks, used by permission of the estate of Roger Duncan.

Designed and produced by
Maine Authors Publishing
558 Main Street
Rockland, Maine 04841
www.maineauthorspublishing.com

Printed in the United States of America

To the loving memory of my parents,

Bob and Lyn Proctor,

and all the people whose lives have wrapped around Pemaquid.

Contents

Downwind From Pemaquid

There are lots of fears hiding in the shadows of Pemaquid, this northern frontier of the New World. But the element most fearsome to me is fire. I know that it can warm us and cook our food. But it can also kill us.

The other thing I don't like to see is blood.

Chapter 1

I am glad that Mother has taught me to read and write, so that I can record these terrible events on the pages of my journal. It is July of 1676, and we are living for the ninth year in a coastal settlement that used to be called Aldridge Town. Now the place is named "Pemaquid," which, in the Penobscot language, means "point of land."

This morning I was working in my mother's herb garden near the door, cutting camomile and feverfew to dry in the rafters. Although I am not quite thirteen, I have learned much about the medicinal uses of herbs from Mother. Camomile leaves, I know, can relieve toothache, stomachache, and diarrhea. The petals of feverfew can cure fever and repel insects. It is also helpful to women in childbirth. Mother will be needing it one of these days, soon.

I turned for a moment and glanced toward the edge of the clearing. Six tall Indians were trading with four of our English colonists under the elm tree. Father was not among them. He was out on the bay with his mates, fishing for cod as he does every day during the summer months. The tall men were our friends the Wawenocks, I knew. During the years we have been here, we have become accustomed to seeing them often in our midst. Today they stood silent and serious, dressed in deerskin, with large piles of beaver pelts stacked on the ground near their feet. Our men were waving their arms sternly, and it seemed as if the trade was going badly. I slid the herbs into my apron pocket and ambled up the hill nearer to them, close enough to hear their voices, but not close enough to be noticed. From the words I overheard, I learned that our men were refusing to trade gunpowder or guns to the Indians for their fine, thick beaver skins.

"Hannah!" my mother called from our doorstep down the hill. I knew she thought it unseemly for women to involve themselves in trade, so I stepped back and headed home. As I turned, I cast a look over my shoulder and spotted a young Indian boy standing behind the group. And just before I headed down the hill, my eye caught a swift movement. It was an older girl—dark and slender, dressed in deerskin, waiting in the shadow of the spruce trees at the edge of the woods.

Chapter 2

"**H**annah! Come quick!" My mother was shouting with some urgency. She was not calling me home because it was improper for me to be near the men's trading. It was an emergency. When I reached the doorway, I glimpsed Mother at the wooden chest where she keeps her medicinals. She quickly stuffed her cloth bag with rags, lamb's ear, yarrow, and some other leaves. Then she motioned me to hurry after her as she ran down the shore toward the fishing station and drying racks. Running was difficult for her, with her large belly, heavy with child.

There at the water's edge lay a man covered with blood and fish scales. Other men hovered around him, some kneeling over him to help, some standing with aimless curiosity. I felt strange approaching the men, because it had always been a rule in my family that I stay far removed from the ruffians working on the shore. They were a young rough bunch of ordinary seamen from the old country, often fighting or drinking. Some of them had served time in jail back in England.

"William!" Mother gasped when we drew near.

I was shocked. The man lying on the sand was my father's younger brother, who had just arrived to work in Pemaquid this year, and lived in our house with us. My first thought was that his hot temper had led him into another violent argument. But it had been an accident. Someone explained in a hurry that his fish knife had slipped as he worked on the cod, and made a deep gash in his forearm.

Mother instructed me to push down on his arm above the wound to stop the bleeding. She yanked some rags from her cloth bag and pressed down. Crimson blood was pulsing out of his arm, but it was slowing as I pressed firmly with my two slippery hands. Mother quickly mixed together a poultice of lamb's ear, yarrow, and moss. She threw it down hard on the wound and leaned on it till the streaming blood slowed even more. Soon it no longer flowed in the rhythm of William's heart. After what seemed like hours but was only minutes, the poultice soaked up the blood, and Mother wrapped more rags tightly around his arm.

The men from the trading party had run down from the hill and swarmed around the group. Before too long, they lifted William shakily to his feet and helped him hobble to our house with Mother. I stood up and glanced down at myself. My hands, apron, and frock were smeared with blood. A wave of dizziness swept over me. I sank down heavily on the sand and retched.

Two figures cast shadows over me. It was the native boy and the tall, dark girl, standing silently beside me. Without a word, the girl led me to the shore, waded in with her deerskin moccasins soaking wet, scooped up the seawater in her cupped hands, and gently washed the blood from my hands and arms.

"You go to your house now," she said quietly.

I staggered blindly toward home, and the two figures faded into the woods.

Chapter 3

Early Fishing Station

William's arm would not be useful for some weeks because of the careless slip of his knife. He had just come over from England to work in the fish station as a shoreman. His job was to cut and salt the cod that my father and other fishermen unloaded from their shallops. William and other men worked for the station manager, Mr. Sewall, who in turn works for the proprietor, a businessman named Abraham Shurt.

The station master bosses the fishermen, carpenters, coopers, and blacksmith, as well as the fish cutters, everyone who works to maintain the fishing station. The largest structure in the station is the fishing stage, which is a large wooden structure without a roof, set on pilings that extend out into the shallow water of Pemaquid Harbor. There is some shelter on the wharf, which has a roof and open sides. A short distance from the stage, just above the high tide mark, there are wooden flakes. They are a series of rectangular planks that look like open frames of tables, covered with spruce boughs and birch bark. Here, shoremen spread the fish to dry in the air after processing. There are also large wooden vats used to cure cod livers for cod liver oil. The men collect seawater from tidal pools to make salt for preserving the sliced fish. Father has no part in the shoremen's work. He sails offshore in the shallops, catching fish with a hand line.

Now, after his accident, Will cannot use a knife, nor can he plunge his arm into the vats of cod liver oil. He cannot even plow the cod waste into the garden as fertilizer. He is not really fit to do any man's work in Pemaquid. Father is disgusted with him. "Life here is hard enough without a stupid mistake," he muttered. "Now we have an extra mouth to feed and you're unable to pull your own weight in the family."

Will offered to move into Shurt's communal building that provides storage and also sleeping quarters for unmarried men who work at the fish station. But Mother wouldn't hear of it, and so he remains in our small house with us, crowded as it is.

There are over a hundred people living in Colonial Pemaquid now, but only twenty small households here in the village, as well as a cluster of single men. Our house is a small earthfast dwelling, framed in hardwood with a floor of boards sitting on piles of stones. The outer walls are covered by wattle-and-daub—woven sticks plastered over with mud, plant fiber, and animal dung. There is not room enough for a person to stand up under the floor, but we can keep some root vegetables and a little smoked meat down there in the cool darkness. Our neighbors, the Earthys, have a well dug into their cellar stones, but we do not, so we share a well with the Gardners. Our roof is made of thatch. Our family lives together in one room. Father and Mother have a bed with a cradle next to it. Uncle William and I both have straw pallets on the floor, in two corners of the room. It is smoky, smelly, and we can all hear each other snore.

The next morning, as I wandered into the edge of the woods scavenging for herbs, the dark girl emerged from the shadows and approached me. She was a handsome young person, with bright brown eyes, high cheek bones, and glowing golden skin. Her waist-long black hair was twisted into a tight, shiny braid woven into a bright-red strip of cloth. Although she was taller than I, I guessed her to be within a year or two of my own age. Unsmiling, she reached out and offered me something. It was a handful of leaves and white blossoms. I recognized it as yarrow, which Mother grows in her garden.

"For the man who was bleeding from the knife," she explained in a soft voice. I thanked her. She backed into the woods with silent footsteps, and that was the last I saw of her for a month. How could I ever have known what part she would play in our little family's struggle to save our lives?

Chapter 4

A party of Wawenock men appeared at the top of the hill a few days later. One of them, a tall, dignified man, seemed to lead the others out of the forest. Master Sewall and two other men from Pemaquid strode up to greet them, and they all walked together to the tavern dooryard to talk. I couldn't hear their words, but the discussion appeared to be courteous. They did not enter the building, but stood outside.

Lingering behind, in the shadows of the trees, were the Indian boy and girl. When I beckoned to them, they stepped out into the sunlight. The boy was tall and muscular, with a very serious air about him. His black hair was pulled smoothly behind his neck and tied with something, perhaps a leather string. He wore a skirt-like garment of animal skin, open at both sides, but no shirt. On his feet there were knee-high leather moccasins, and above them his legs were uncovered. His bare skin was the color of tanned deer hide. He was very clean. I guessed him to be older than the girl by one or two years. I extended my hand in friendship, but they seemed unfamiliar with our custom, and did not reach out to me.

"I am glad to see you in our village," I said.

For the first time, I heard the boy speak. "Our people hunt many deer herds here before you white people come."

I thanked him for allowing us to build homes here on their land, and fish the sea.

He replied, "No one owns the land. It can be used by all people... Wawenock, Penobscot, or Englishmen. The animals in the forest belong to no one but themselves. The great harvest of the sea—cod, elvers, sturgeon, oysters, shad—they are there for all of us to catch and eat, for our need." Then he told me that we newcomers in Pemaquid had built our

15

village at the mouth of their carrying place from the other side of the peninsula. For thousands of moons, in summertime their people had traveled up and down the coast in canoes laden with beaver, otter, and marten skins to trade. They had carried their canoes out of the water and walked overland along a path they had made, to avoid the rough waters around the rocky and stormy point of land north of our settlement.

I told him that we English people had begun to use that portage path as an ox and wagon road. "Are you Wawenock people?" I asked them.

The girl replied, "We are of the Penobscot tribe, part of the Abenaki Nation. "

"The French call us 'Etchemen,'" her brother added. "We are here with our grandfather, Madockawando. Our people are here to join the Wawenocks and speak together with the Englishmen."

"You speak very good English," I commented.

"Our French words are better," replied the boy. He ended the conversation, turned, and ambled down the hill in long strides to the cove.

"He goes to see if there are mussels on the shore," the girl told me. "The English build dams and sawmills on the river that rushes to the sea. Englishmen stop the alewives who run up the rivers. No more do they lay eggs in the ponds above the rivers of many fishes." She lowered herself into a sitting position, cross-legged in the grass. "We wait here for Madockawando."

I followed her example, and sat down facing her. "What are your names?" I ventured.

"He is called Bernard-Anselme. I am Claire. How are you called?" she asked.

I was surprised. "I am Hannah," I told her. After a long silence, I asked, "How is it that the grandchildren of Madockawando do not have Penobscot names?" I was thinking that perhaps it was not a polite question.

"Our mother is Madockawando's daughter. In the Abenaki way, women are heads of our families. I think that is not so with white people. But she is married to Baron de San Castin, Chief of Pentagouet, on the north coast. He is our father. He is a white man."

Chapter 5

I lay on my pallet in the dark that night, thinking about what Bernard-Anselme had said. How could it be that English people saved money for passage over here to the New World, cleared the land, built homes and cod stations, paid taxes to King George in England, and did not own the land they lived on? It also confused me that my two new Penobscot friends had French-sounding names. It puzzled my mind until I fell into a troubled, dream-ridden sleep. In my dreams were fire and danger, faceless enemies breaking down our doors at night.

About a month ago, Master Thomas Gardner had explained the problem to the families in our settlement. The Wawenocks and Penobscots are members of the Mawoochen Confederacy for trading with the English and French colonists. They trade beaver, marten, and other skins for useful items that we can give them. There are different grades of beaver pelts, some more valuable than others. The Indians will trade one good-quality beaver skin for six fathoms of tobacco string. They like woven cloth, too, and sometimes army uniforms, if anyone has them. They especially value tools and weapons made of metal. Six knives are worth one beaver skin to them. Now the issue of argument has shifted. The Indians want guns and ammunition.

At dusk the next afternoon, Madockawando came once again to our clearing with five or six Wawenock and Penobscot men to negotiate with our English men. I don't know why I was allowed to stand in the back of the meeting at Earthy's Tavern. My chores were finished, and I was able to squeeze in against the rear wall near the door. There was so much commotion that no one noticed me. It was hot and smoky there, and the crowded room reeked of sweat. It seemed as if almost all the members of the village were there, even though mothers with small children stayed at home.

I was glad that Mother had reminded me to wear my tussy mussy. A tussy mussy is a lace doily, tied up with ribbon and filled with sage flower and lavender. We hang it around our necks to improve the smell of the air in a long, crowded meeting, with the press of bodies in a small space. We English people bathe only once a year, if at all, but I'm told that the Indians wash their bodies every day. This seems hard to believe, considering the cold climate here.

The meeting between the Indians and our people seemed to be going badly, and tempers were rising. There were fearful rumors of Abenaki attacks on villages south of Pemaquid. This seemed amazing to me because we had always considered the Indian people our friends. However, we learned that most of the English settlers along the coast have been unwilling to let them have weapons, and this is the reason for the rumors of attack.

Two of the Wawenock men spoke angrily to Madockawando and he translated their words for the Englishmen.

"English men are cutting down the forests so the deer, who feed us, run far away. So, too, they dam the rivers for their sawmills, and the fish swim up the falls no more. Our people will starve this winter." Madockawando stood tall and straight, and spoke in a dignified voice, but he could not calm a serious argument that erupted.

Master Thomas Gardner stood up for the Wawenocks. "The Wawenocks are loyal to us, and we need to reward their friendship with kindness. Last winter they had difficulty feeding their people without powder to use in their hunting. I do not know very much about Madockawando and the Penobscots, but they have come to help the Wawenocks negotiate."

I could not hear the words clearly, and was unable to follow the discussion after that. Before it went very far, though, my Uncle William slipped through the door, his injured arm in a sling, and summoned me outside into the foggy night air.

"You must come home now," he urged quietly. "Emma's time is here."

That was my mother. Her labor had begun.

Chapter 6

I hastened to our house and found Mother on her side in bed. My grandmother's quilt had been thrown off, and she was covered by homespun cotton cloth. Her face was red and shiny with sweat, reflecting the light from the oil lamp. Mistress Gardner was with her, bustling around with linen cloths. She was pouring pots of water from the cauldron that hung from the fireplace spit, and the small room was filled with steam. Mistress Gardner and my mother have been midwives in our village for about nine years, which is as long as I can remember, but my mother is known to have the better skill with medicinal herbs. In spite of my young age, I, too, have assisted at births on two occasions before this, and Mother has taught me much.

As soon as I entered the house, William departed and joined my father at the meeting in Earthy Tavern.

Mother's labor was progressing swiftly, for this was her fifth confinement, and babies come more quickly after the first one. I was her first child, having been born in England before my parents set off for the New World. The midwife there was able to give Mother laudanum, a potent painkiller made from opium seeds and cooked with other herbs. Unfortunately, this medicine is not available here in Pemaquid. Lizzie, my first sister, was stillborn. The next child, Hattie, lived only one day, and Jonathan died of fever the following winter at the age of one month, six days. All three are buried in the village cemetery in Pemaquid, at the top of the hill near the harbor. Their little graves are marked by wooden crosses but have no names upon them. They may not last, unfortunately, as long as a generation. Some of our neighbors have marked their family graves with rough round stones carried up from the shore. We have no stonecutters among us here. We have no minister here, either, to lead us in prayer or hymns But all of our families have personal Bibles, and at each burial, Father read some words from ours.

Mother began panting. I sat beside her, holding a cool wet cloth to her forehead. I was also instructed to feed her two spoonfuls of feverfew, which had been cooked in honey, to speed along the contractions. Then she was holding my hand hard and squeezing it till I thought my fingers would break off. She uttered a few loud animal sounds like grunts, and the baby popped out, red, wet, and slippery, into Mistress Gardner's hands! I leaned over to peek at the tiny creature—a girl. She was very, very small, not as large as other newborn babies I have seen. And she didn't breathe.

Mistress Gardner held her upside down, cleared her mouth out with her finger, and shook her up and down. She slapped her on the back several times, and then again on her chest. There was a gurgling sound and then a sputter. At last, the baby gave a weak little cough and then came a sound like a kitten mewing. She was alive! Mother lifted her head, looked at the child, and smiled weakly.

Mistress Gardner wiped her off, wrapped her in clean cotton cloth, and told me to lay her on Mother's breast.

"This child shall be called Sarah," Mother said.

Chapter 7

SWH

The days seem longer than ever now. I realize that it is August, and the sun stays high in the sky for longer hours than it did months ago. But Mother has to rest in bed for many long days, and I have been in full charge of the household for more than a fortnight. Father works long hours and William has only one useful arm to help. There is so much to do.

First, I must tend to Mother in her bed and baby Sarah in her cradle. That means emptying the chamber pot into the privy in the back of the house, changing the baby's clouts, washing both Mother and Sarah with rags, and bringing Mother some gruel. It is fortunate that Mother's milk has come in, and has been enough to feed the baby for the time being. Soon Sarah will be ready to eat gruel, and other foods, too, I hope.

Now, it is a month after Sarah's birth. Even though it is summer, I need to keep the fire going endlessly in the large open fireplace for heating water and cooking. There must be a kettle always hanging from the lugpole. That means we need armloads of firewood and kindling every day. William has tried to help carry wood in every day despite his injured arm, but he cannot split logs one-handedly with an ax. That means Father has to do the wood-splitting after he gets home from the fishery, late in the day while the sun is setting. William goes out with the buckets to the well we share with the Gardner family, and with difficulty, he can shovel up dung for the manure pile using his one good arm.

I tend our handful of chickens and collect their eggs from the coop. I take turns milking the four cows that six of our families tend together. Several of our girls and women share this work. Lizzie Gardner is the nearest to me in age, but she is only ten, three years younger than me, and not big enough to help me with women's work. She is definitely not old enough to share secrets. I don't really want to tell her about Bernard-Anselme and Claire. I have been gathering carrots, turnips, and greens from our garden, saving some of the turnips for Bess, my favorite cow. I hardly have time to weed the vegetable garden or the herbs anymore. I am hoping that the squash will ripen before it is too late. Winters are very harsh here in Pemaquid, but I can keep squash from freezing by covering it with sawdust and soil under the floor. I have learned to mix, knead, and bake bread twice a week. I try to churn butter when I get a chance, but it is a tedious task, and makes my back ache something terrible.

During the last few years, I have helped Mother and learned how to stew chicken, fish, and vegetables. If the men shot a deer, I learned how to roast venison on a spit over the fire, turning it around and around for hours, with the fat dripping down into a pan beneath it. There is never-ending washing and mending, and knitting of stockings, but I never seem to have enough time for it all.

This week I suffered a troublesome accident. The lugpole dried out and snapped. It is a green branch stretching over the fire, fitted into two small holes in the opposite sides of the fireplace. One day it dropped the heavy kettle of stew down into the fire with a loud crash, splattering stew and red-hot sparks out onto the hearth. Some of the sparks ignited my skirt and petticoat. No one was at home except Mother and Baby Sarah in the bed, so I had to beat out the flames at my ankles with a shovel. Mother laid the baby aside and jumped from the bed to come to my aid. Finally, I was able to reach the water basin and pour it all over my knees and feet.

When it was all over, I stripped the burnt stockings, shoes, and tattered petticoat from my legs. My skin was blistered and peeling. Mother found some comfrey and aloe to mix with butter, and smoothed it over the destroyed skin. We wrapped clean rags around my terrible red legs up to my knees.

But these were not our biggest problems. The worst issue we have to deal with is that, just a month after her birth, baby Sarah is ill.

Chapter 8

Since the day of her birth, Sarah has uttered soft little coughs. She sleeps fitfully and cries restlessly most of the night. Her face is flushed and her small body is often hot. Mother has been giving her tiny mouthfuls of tea mixed with feverfew, which seem to cool down her skin and quiet her somewhat. At night I take turns carrying her around the room or humming to her while I swing back and forth in the rocking chair. I am very afraid that we will lose her, like the other babies before.

This morning Mother rummaged through the cloth bag in her wooden chest and brought out a small glass bottle half full of a thick, dark-purple syrup.

"This is elderberry tonic," she told me. "It is strong medicine that can fight many bad diseases." She wrapped a tiny bundle of sugar in a piece of clean muslin and tied it tightly with thread. She poured about three drops of the berry tonic into a small dish, being ever so careful not to spill any of the valuable liquid, and soaked the cotton-wrapped sugar with it. Then she touched it to Sarah's little pink mouth and the baby sucked softly on it. I took her from Mother and held her for a while until she closed her eyes, and then I laid her gently into her cradle.

This was the first quiet morning we had had in more than a fortnight. Father had taken his hand lines and gone out early in a shallop with some other men to fish close to shore. William had drifted down to the harbor to see if he could be of any use to the men working on the drying racks.

By afternoon, I was overcome by intense weariness. My arms and back ached, and my eyes were heavy. Mother was up and moving around strongly now. She busied herself with a stew of beans, squash, and chicken broth that was beginning to bubble in the kettle over the fire.

She touched my arm. "You have been working too hard for so long, Hannah," she said. "Why don't you lie down and rest for a spell, to get some strength back?"

I protested weakly, but she insisted. So I eased myself down to my straw pallet on the floor in the corner, and slept heavily for several hours that I did not count.

The late-August afternoon sun came slanting through the open door when I awoke to Sarah's little choking cries. Mother was measuring out another dose of the elderberry tonic to give to the baby. She held the bottle up to rays of sunshine in the doorway. I was alarmed to see that the medicine was almost gone.

"Hannah," she said quietly but with some urgency, "take this bottle over to Mistress Earthy and Mistress Gardner to see if they have any elderberry tonic to spare us."

Without questioning, I jumped to my feet, threw the quilt over my pallet, and pushed it back against the wall. Then I quickly took the little bottle from Mother's hand and hurried out the door.

I could not find Mistress Earthy in her house next to her husband's tavern, so I ran around to the back garden, where she was moving up and down the rows, harvesting squash.

"Alas, my girl," she sighed, "I ran out of the tonic last winter. I could not find any elderberry patches this year. With the rainy spring we had, I think perhaps we will not see any elderberries this fall."

Next I hurried up the hill toward the woods where the Gardners lived. Lizzie was sitting in the doorway trying to darn a sock, without much success, from the looks of it. She was eager to drop the irksome task and take me to her mother, who was kneading bread dough on the table. She, too, explained that it was too early for this year's elderberries to ripen, and was disappointed to have no tonic left over from last year. Weary with despair, I left their house and collapsed in the grass at the edge of the woods. After a moment, I was startled by a quiet footfall nearby, and turned in surprise to see Claire standing in the shadows. Bernard-Anselme was standing quietly farther back in the woods.

Ashamed to have them notice a tear trickling down my cheek, I wiped my face hastily with my apron. At that quick motion, the little bottle fell out of my pocket and a drop of the precious liquid spilled out onto my apron. In haste, I tried to scoop up the tiny drop with my finger and broke into tears. Claire reached down, touched the purple drop with her finger, and sniffed it. Then she held it to her brother's nose as he stepped out from the shade of the trees. He named it with a word I did not know, not "elderberry," but some Indian word.

"I need the juice from this berry to cure my baby sister's sickness," I told them. "Do you know where it grows?"

"It grows in the hills, far from this place," Bernard-Anselme replied. "It turns ripe in the time our people pack up our homes and travel to our winter hunting ground."

"When is that?" I leaped up, desperate for his words. I should have remembered that the Wawenocks and Penobscots left this area sometime in the autumn every year.

"Two moons from this one," he answered. Two months! This was August. The elderberries would not be ripe until October. For Sarah, perhaps that would be too late. I held the little bottle up to the sun, which was sinking over the western shore across the bay. There was very little liquid left in the bottom.

Although the Penobscots do not show emotion the way we English do, Claire could see that I was very, very upset. "Our mother mashes these berries and dries them flat on birch bark," she said. "Our people keep them, use them in winter, summer, both times, all times."

I leaped up in wild excitement. "Oh, Claire, do you think we could get some of these dried berries from your mother, so we could make this tonic to cure my baby sister?"

Claire and Bernard looked at each other doubtfully. "She lives many days from this place," answered Bernard, "a place called Pentagouet."

"We come now to bid you farewell," Claire told me. "We go back to Pentagouet with Madockawando and his men."

"But why? Why are you going away so soon?" I cried out.

"Our people and your people no more trade together. No talking more," Bernard answered quietly. "Our people and your people are friends many moons. King Philip's War is coming to this place. Now we are friends no more forever. So we go." Bernard-Anselme and Claire both raised their right hands, palms facing me.

"But wait! I don't understand! Who is King Philip?" I cried hopelessly.

My two friends turned without another word and disappeared into the forest. I walked slowly down the hill to my home. My hand clutched the apron pocket that held what little was left of the precious tonic.

Chapter 9

1675 Shallop

As I dragged myself wearily home, I was suddenly aware of a wild commotion in the village. Everyone was running to Earthy's Tavern: Father, William, Mother, and the baby, all the Gardners and everybody else were crowding through the door. Alarmed, I pushed my way inside, past the neighbors, and huddled next to my family. Baby Sarah was shrieking in fright. All the adults were chattering and shouting at once. At the front of the room, a young woman sat, exhausted, on a stool, gulping a cup of water. Her clothes were torn, her hair was flying loose, and her bare feet were bleeding. Someone had given her a blanket to cover her shaking shoulders. I was stunned and frightened at the sight of her.

Mr. Earthy banged on the counter for quiet and spoke to us. "This is Mistress Dollen from Sheepscot. She has been running for two and a half days to bring us some terrible news. She was alone at her homestead outside Sheepscot Village, her father and mother having some business at Pemaquid Falls. Young Thomas of the Giles family came running up her path in great agitation."

Between gasps of breath, Mistress Dollen recovered enough to continue with the story. "Thomas came running from the Sagadahock region, south of the Kennebec River. He shouted for me to flee for my life because the Abenakis were working their way up the coast, attacking farmsteads in the middle of the night. They were killing almost everyone and putting torches to the dwellings. He could see white smoke in the southern sky. He told me a large number of Indians overran his farmhouse at break of day. His father tried to shoot his musket, but he was outnumbered, and his parents were slain as they ran from their home. He told me the only reason he escaped was that he had gone out at dawn to tend his traps in the river. I ran and tried to find my parents at Pemaquid Falls, but they were gone." Then she broke down and cried uncontrollably.

There was a sudden strange silence in the tavern, then loud, confusing voices again. Mr. Earthy banged a spoon on the counter for attention, and Mr. Thomas Gardner jumped up beside him. Mr. Gardner is an officer of the Devonshire County Court, and the nearest thing to a military officer here in Pemaquid. He has a commanding voice.

"Last year I made a long journey to Boston to oppose the Massachusetts policy of keeping powder and shot from the Indians, who needed it for winter hunting. I tried to convince them that we had a peaceful relationship with the Wawenocks here on the coast. But the Boston politicians accused me of illegally selling powder and shot to the Indians. I could have ended in jail, but I finally cleared myself of that charge. Unfortunately, our delegation achieved nothing else. Now it is too late."

People in the tavern began to shout now. A couple of women seemed close to hysterics. Mr. Earthy had to quiet the crowd yet again so that Mr. Gardner could continue.

"Our lives are sorely in danger. I recommend that we load all the shallops on the shore with whatever necessities we can gather for our immediate use, tonight in the darkness. We must pray that the Abenakis do not advance within the next few hours. At sunrise, we can sail on the northwest wind ten miles down John's Bay to Damariscove Island. There has been a cod station established there for some fifty or more years. There is a large freshwater pond. It is far enough from land, surrounded by rough ocean water, to prevent the Indians from approaching in canoes. I believe we can find safety there."

There was a little excited discussion, but not much. It seemed obvious to all that an escape by land would not be fast enough for us to survive an attack. Our only desperate route was by sea. The tavern emptied out quickly and we all scattered to our homes to throw together whatever we could think we might need in a run for our lives. *Damariscove Island...where is that?* I knew not, and was bewildered.

We were terrified when we dashed into our home. Where to begin? We never anticipated leaving this place ever, much less in a few hours, gathering belongings before dark! Father and William began by hauling two barrels up from the shore, used for salting cod, and smelling strongly of fish. Father threw in a bag of tools, fishing hand lines, jiggers, and hooks. William added two fish knives and some canvas. Mother got them to lift in a heavy sack of flour. She calmly gathered up the baby's needs, her valuable box of medicines, spoons and four trenchers, and the cooking pot with some stew left in it after we had each had a few mouthfuls. I collected and put in some quilts for bedding, warm cloaks, thread, and needles. I hated the thought of packing our bedding and clothing in the foul-smelling cod barrel. Last of all, I slipped in my diary. We were able to place, on the top of the barrel, a basket containing two of our hens, who protested loudly.

We regretted desperately what we had to leave behind. We could not take the four cows. I ran out to hug and kiss Bess, my special favorite, and gave her some sweet salt-marsh grass from Pemaquid Falls as a final treat. What would become of the poor creatures? The Gardners intended, somehow, to bring along a nanny goat, but I did not know how she could fit into one of the boats with all the other goods and people. I was so sad to leave the eight new apple trees we had nursed along behind the kitchen garden for two years. I remember when I was eleven helping to dig the holes to plant them with cow manure, and patting the mounds around their little roots. I could picture them in flames when the Abenakis came with fiery torches. With unspeakable sorrow, I thought of our three little graves in the cemetery up on the hill.

Darkness came too soon, but none of us slept. Father and William kept running among the houses in the village, making last-minute plans in hushed voices. Mother, Sarah, and I huddled in the darkened house, awake until dawn.

Before sunrise, everyone was down at the shore, running back one more time for items remembered as necessities. At last, we were loaded into the shallops, pushed off and floating quietly in the harbor, waiting for the tide to turn and run out through the narrow gut at the mouth. This is the place of reversing waters, as the Wawenocks call it, where the current turns on itself with the tide. No men's oars or sails can fight it. So we had to wait.

After a long, silent wait, the ripples finally reversed direction and the men pulled on the oars to get us through. They raised the sails, the early morning breeze slowly rose from the northwest, and at last we glided out toward the open ocean and Damariscove. The hot August sun rose. With the blessing of the morning breeze, the shallops glided slowly downwind from Pemaquid.

Chapter 10

As we drew near to Damariscove Isle, we could see that it was actually two small islands joined by a sandbar. The southern end was a high bluff, and then it sloped to sea level on the north, facing the distant mainland. There were many puffs of smoke all over the island, probably from cook fires. The wind carried foul odors toward our boats: the stench of rotting fish and excrement, as from uncovered privies. This mixed with the unpleasant odors aboard our shallop, caused by some of our people who had been overcome by seasickness. Sarah was coughing. I wished I had brought my tussy mussy.

The sun was not quite at the highest point of the sky when our boats rounded the southern headland of Damariscove Isle. I shielded my eyes and gazed back toward Pemaquid Harbor, the place that used be our village. All that I had known was gone forever. I half expected to see spreading fire and smoke rising, but the sky over the mainland was still clear and blue. For a moment, I thought there had been some horrible mistake, that everything was a bad dream that could not be happening.

Large rolling ocean waves heaved us into the narrow little south-facing harbor on Damariscove. All sails were dropped, and our nine boats ground to a stop on the coarse gravel. We were shocked at what we saw. The little island, about two miles long and barely a quarter-mile wide, was covered by humanity and debris. There were all sizes of boats along the shore—in the water, on the gravel, and dragged up into the weeds. Some had been pulled apart for their wood or upturned for rude shelters. At the head of the harbor was a careless excuse for a cod station—old, rotten, and in need of repair.

Smoke rose from cook fires, whipped by the brisk offshore wind.

Tents were fashioned from tattered sails. Scrap wood was arranged as makeshift dwellings. Scores of men, women, and children were crowded into every square meter of space. There was a heavy stench of rotten fish and human waste. The air was full of shouts and the cries of babies. In spite of the strong sun high in the midday sky, there was a cold ocean wind that brought an omen of winter.

When we stepped ashore, there seemed to be almost no trees. Any grass that remained was trampled. Father and William joined some other men and set out to search for the freshwater pond, if indeed there really was one. We women of the Pemaquid families huddled nervously together near all our supplies in the shallops, keeping our distance from so many strangers. Sarah cried weakly.

Chapter 11

The men returned in early afternoon with discouraging news. "There are refugees here from as far away as the Sheepscot and Kennebec Rivers," Father said. "They are all escaping from the Indian attacks."

"We are told that there are close to three hundred souls camping here," Mr. Earthy added. "There is a freshwater pond, but it is quickly becoming fouled."

Another man said, "What few privies were here are overflowing with filth."

"The only food is what people have brought with them, or what can be caught in the sea. There are no birds or animals here to shoot," said Father. "If there ever were plants to eat, none are left."

Mother sighed and handed the baby to me. "We have some chicken stew in a pot that we packed in a barrel. If some of us can salvage wood for a fire, we all can have a share of it."

"Alas," Mrs. Gardner replied, "Lizzie and I have been combing the shore for driftwood or pieces of broken boats, but the island has been picked clean." Two little boys from the Earthy family reported that they had climbed up above the grass line and found no firewood of any kind.

We few families bravely scraped together some cold food gathered in haste from our homes in Pemaquid, and we shared what we had. Thank goodness Mother has breast milk for Sarah. But at the age of one month, the poor baby still coughs and wheezes. And the bottle of elderberry tonic is empty now. Mother keeps Sarah constantly wrapped tightly to her breast in a warm shawl. We prepared to sleep under canvas and cloaks in our boats, pulled up on the gravel, and to guard what goods we had brought with us. Then we huddled together for a conference.

"I think we must empty two boats and take a party of men back to Pemaquid to gather more supplies," Mr. Gardner declared. "We cannot live here on what meager goods we brought with us this morning."

"Whoever goes back will be risking their lives," Mrs. Earthy protested. "We are told that the Abenakis have been attacking villages at night and burning them down!"

A wave of fear washed over me.

Father thought for a few minutes and suggested, "Perhaps if we move swiftly, there is a little time left for us to go back to Pemaquid and gather up more foodstuffs that we sorely need to survive."

Another man added, "The prevailing wind in summer fetches up from the south after noontime. It could carry two boats almost up John's Bay to Pemaquid, before it dies at nightfall. Then we could use our oars to carry us into the harbor under darkness."

It was decided to draw straws and six men would make the dangerous journey. William wanted to draw one of the straws, but he was refused. A young man with only one-and-a-half strong arms would not be useful during a long row the last few miles, or to load the boats in the dark.

The straws were drawn and the names were read out: "Giles, McFarland, Sewall, Blaisdell, Gardner, Brown." I gasped and covered my mouth. Brown is our name.

"Oh no, Father!" I whispered.

Chapter 12

Everyone moved as swiftly as possible to unload goods from two of the shallops and stack them on the gravel close to the other seven boats.

"See if you can salvage some of the dried meat and vegetables from under the house, Israel," Mother urged Father, "and if you can, bring a few more hens."

Mistress Gardner wondered whether they could find room for one more goat. Others asked for a barrel of salted fish, or even some buckets of salt alone. There were other hasty requests for firewood and tools. A few men asked for gunpowder and shot from the storehouse.

Is it possible to get a cow into one boat? I wondered, thinking of my poor Bess, left behind.

Before we could think any more carefully about the plan, the six men had shoved off and were headed out of the harbor. I climbed up the bluff with Lizzie and the two Earthy boys. We watched the sails fill as they glided up John's Bay. The sky over Pemaquid was still clear and blue. No sign of smoke.

I was very frightened.

As we watched, three more boats arrived from the south with colonists running from danger. How could such a small island hold any more refugees? It was unbelievably crowded.

Just about sunset, I glimpsed a lone sailing vessel approaching from the northern mainland. This seemed strange to me, because most of the boats fleeing from danger were sailing in from the west. As the craft drew nearer to the harbor, I strained to get a look at the three occupants. They were a white sailor dressed in britches and jacket, and two dark-skinned young people—a young man and a girl. I stared in disbelief. It couldn't be, but it was. Claire and Bernard-Anselme!

I ran as fast as lightning down to the shore to greet them. I fell once, and picked myself up just as the boat scraped up over the gravel. The sailor let the sails luff. Bernard hopped out and held the boat steady while Claire climbed over the side, soaking her moccasins in the water.

"How did you know we were here?" I said, almost stuttering in astonishment.

Neither of them answered. Claire reached up and removed a deer skin pouch that was hanging on a leather sinew over one shoulder and diagonally down to her waist on the opposite side. She reached out and gave it to me.

"What is this?" I asked, puzzled. I opened the pouch carefully and drew out a small clear bottle, its lid sealed with wax. It contained a thick purple liquid. Under it, at the bottom of the pouch, was another just like it. The elderberry tonic! I choked back tears and could not speak.

"Our mother sends it to you for the bébé," Claire said. Then she turned, and without another word, jumped back aboard. Swiftly, Bernard swung the boat around, hopped aboard, and the sailor began to row out of the harbor. I was astounded.

"But wait!" I shouted, finding my voice at last. "How can I thank her?" I wished I had something to give them...perhaps my looking glass or comb or something, but then I remembered that I had left those things behind in Pemaquid. And perhaps Claire and Bernard might have been insulted.

"We go now," Claire said simply. She and Bernard held up their palms to me.

The sailor called back gruffly, "These young people are not safe on this shore. We must head back to Pentagouet. They started out to this cursed island alone by canoe, but the Baron de Castin ordered them into my sailboat to cross the open water. He will kill me if I do not bring them back alive!"

The boat rolled once as it rounded the bluff at the harbor mouth and rode up over the frothing waves of the open sea. I looped the string of the pouch around my neck, shielded my eyes with one hand and waved wildly with the other.

"Thank you, thank you! Goodbye," I called as the last rays of the sunlight turned their sail into a distant shadow on the darkening sea. Wiping a tear from my wet face, I clutched the leather pouch with its priceless medicine tight to my chest, and hurried back to Mother and the neighbors.

Chapter 13

We ate cold soup and stale bread. We tried to sleep in the open air or under canvas, curled up against the boats. It was a long, terrible, sleepless night. There were voices, loud and soft, everywhere around us, some quite near. There were children crying. Sarah has been quiet because of the elderberry tonic and echinacea. Mother has been so grateful for the medicine. She and I had snuggled Sarah up in woolen shawls, and she lay between us.

Mother worries about the rough men on the codfish teams. Some came over to this New World to escape prison sentences in England for fighting or stealing. I suspect that Uncle William might have been one of them, but I am not sure. Mother and Father have talked about him in whispers, away from my hearing.

What is to become of us? What is happening now to Father and the five other men who returned to the village to salvage some more necessities? These thoughts filled my mind as I lay sleepless on the shore. Lookouts took turns on the bluff with a spyglass left behind by Mr. Gardner when he set out on the dangerous mission at the last minute.

Dawn was not bright. A dull haze covered the sky. While Mother nursed Sarah, I dashed up to the bluff to look toward Pemaquid with many of the others. WHITE SMOKE! It was billowing high into the lightening sky. The bitter smell was blowing downwind from Pemaquid. Angry flames of red and orange were spreading along the shoreline, with sparks shooting high up into the air. I thought of the fire that had burned my leg when the lugpole broke and the pot fell into the fireplace. How severe that hurt was! What would it feel like to burn to death? As I stood there on the rise of Damariscove, looking toward my burning village, I did not know whether my father or any of the other men had suffered an agonizing death! I made a fist of my hand and pounded it over my mouth to keep myself from screaming.

There were several minutes of moaning, weeping, cursing, general confusion among the people. Suddenly a shout went up from Mr. Earthy, who was straining to see through the spyglass, and the shout was echoed by several people standing close to him.

"A sail! I see a sail!" he declared. Others hollered with him, and a cheer went up.

Then one of the little Earthy boys, whose eyes were very keen, announced, "Two! There are two sails! I see two boats!"

The spyglass was rapidly passed from hand to hand and there was much rejoicing all around.

Chapter 14

Autumn 1676

Father and the other men escaped with their lives and a few recovered possessions that dreadful day in August. They loaded the two shallops with all they could collect from the village as the dark descended. Alas, they had to leave the animals behind, and I imagine that the poor creatures perished in the Abenaki attack a few hours later.

The men rowed the two loaded boats out into Pemaquid Harbor in the moonless dark of night and floated silently, waiting for the tide to turn and carry them out through the gut. When the tide finally turned, they were able to help themselves through with silent oars. Finally, the morning northwest breeze rose predictably, they raised their sails, and slowly picked up speed to head down John's Bay.

It was then that the Abenakis attacked our village. There might have been a hundred men, decorated with warpaint and carrying English weapons and flaming torches. Shots were aimed at the two escaping shallops, and Mr. Blaisdell took a gunshot to his shoulder. He bravely announced, "I survived the shipwreck of the *Angel Gabriel*, so I can mighty well recover from this!" Our men fired back with their muskets, but fortunately the winds were fair, and carried them out of range after that.

It was a sad dawn when our men sailed out with what remained of their village possessions and landed in the arms of their families on Damariscove.

Our Pemaquid company remained in the safety of Damariscove Isle for only two days. It was clear to all that there was no space left on that little island for the entire colony of Pemaquid to set up homesteads and exist for the coming winter.

Word came from the cod fishermen that there might be room for us on the island of Monhegan, ten miles farther out at sea. So our families held a meeting and decided to sail out there to improve our chances. I have great hope for our survival. Sarah is growing plump and rosy with no remaining trace of a cough. Mother removed the gunshot pellets from Mr. Blaisdell's shoulder and cleaned it with tincture of yarrow. William is using his arm again, and the rest of us are healthy.

Two memories I will carry with me for the rest of my days—our priceless gift of friendship with the Wawenock and Penobscot people, and the horrifying, deadly smell of smoke downwind from Pemaquid.

Looking Back, Three Years Later

My parents, Israel and Emma Brown, my beautiful little sister Sarah, and I did not remain on Monhegan Island when autumn approached in 1676. There was not enough land, shelter, or food sources to sustain more families there. It was too late in the year to plant a garden, even if we had been able to carry seeds out there with us. The men who fished the summer waters around the island were packing up to return to winter fishing stations along the southern mainland. Their boats, large and small, were headed for the north shore of Boston—the villages of Gloucester, Salem, and Essex. As the weather turned cold, our family joined with others headed that way. After a long, weary sail, we finally made landfall in Marblehead, where we had the good fortune to join a settlement and an established fishing station.

While my father fishes, my mother and I keep house, perform the important work as midwives in the village, and watch our rosy-cheeked Sarah run about with the neighbors' children. My father's brother William stayed behind on Monhegan Island and, in the spring, returned to the Pemaquid Peninsula, where he was able to find work on an inland farm. Eventually he acquired some land of his own in his family name of Brown.

Soon other English fishermen and traders resettled Pemaquid, and it thrived as a new colony called Jamestown. The last we heard was that Bernard-Anselme had become a respected Abenaki chief. I do not know what became of Claire, but I will always carry her memory in my heart as a courageous, strong woman who risked the anger of her tribe and helped us survive.

In my words,
Hannah Brown, Age 15

Partial Time Line
from the Colonial Pemaquid State Historic Site

1625-1629   A permanent, year-round English settlement was established at Pemaquid (exact dates conflict).

1630-1650   Pemaquid was probably at its peak as the English fur trading center in Maine.

1630   Abraham Shurt built a fortified warehouse for trading goods at Pemaquid.

1631   Robert Aldworth and Gyles Elbridge became proprietors of Pemaquid through the Pemaquid Patent.

1635   The ship, *Angel Gabriel*, sank along the coast of Pemaquid during a hurricane, and many passengers survived.

1673-1676   Pemaquid was governed by Massachusetts.

1674   John Earthy's tavern was licensed.

1676   The Pemaquid settlement was destroyed by Native Americans during King Philip's War.

1677   Fort Charles was built and a settlement, called Jamestown after the Duke of York, was reestablished.

Historical Notes

Abraham Shurt Pemaquid Fish Station manager, who built a fortified warehouse and wooden wharves.

Angel Gabriel An English ship destroyed by a hurricane in 1635 at anchor in Pemaquid. Many passengers and crew survived, and their descendants live in the area today.

Baron de St. Castin French military officer serving in Canada who remained in Maine, was adopted by a local tribe, and became an Abenaki chief. He took an Indian wife, daughter of Madockawando, Penobscot sachem.

Claire and Bernard-Anselme Children of Baron de St. Castin and Madockawando's daughter. Bernard grew up to become an Abenaki chief.

Clouts Pieces of cloth used for cleaning, patching, or as baby's diapers.

Earthfast homes Houses that sat directly on the ground, with super-structures of timber frames covered with wattle-and-daub (clay and straw) infill or sometimes wooden clapboards. Roofed with either wooden shingles or thatch, common in Western England, particularly in Devon, 15th-19th centuries. Windows were of wooden frames covered with oiled paper.

Elderberry tonic A medicine used by both colonists and Native Americans as a powerful immune booster, especially for bronchial and other respiratory ailments. Contains concentrated Vitamin C, and is still sold in health food stores today.

John Earthy A sometime "superintendent" of Pemaquid, worked to achieve peace with the Native Americans and established Earthy's Tavern.

Fathom a length of six feet, unit of measure for the depth of water or the length of a rope.

King Phillip's War Colonists' hunger for land, as well as heavy-handed treatment of Wampanoag and other native people by government officials, led to a series of raids and bloody conflicts throughout New England, 1675-76.

Madockawando Born around 1635, a prominent Abenaki sachem of the Penobscot tribe, influenced by the French. He made treaties with the English, which the whites broke. Gave his daughter in marriage to Baron de St. Castin. His grandchildren were Claire and Bernard-Anselm.

Pemaquid One of the nation's earliest and most historically significant English settlements—England's farthest outpost to the northeast; nearest settlement to the French in Acadia.

Pemaquid Patent A royal grant from Bristol, England, to settlers Aldworth and Elbridge, of an area of 12,000 acres from the Damariscotta River east to the Muscongus River.

Penobscots A tribe north of Pemaquid, friendly with the French, whose leaders tried unsuccessfully to make treaties with the English.

Pentagouet (Also Peimtagoet) Area near the mouth of the Penobscot River, a half-day sail from Pemaquid. Acadian fortified outpost, seat of French military government and major trading post with a garrison of 25 troops.

Sachem Among some North American Indian tribes, the chief of the tribe or of a confederation.

Shallops Small open boats fitted with oars and sails, sometimes stabilized by sideboards.

Thomas Gardner Fifteen-year resident of early Pemaquid, with his wife and children. Commissioner, Justice of the Peace, Militia Commander of Devonshire County; leading trader with the Wawenocks and the French.

Trencher A wooden board or platter on which to carve or serve food.

Wawenocks Native Americans who used this land thousands of years before the Europeans. A tribe of the Eastern Abenaki Nation. Had peaceful relationship with the English until treaties were broken and the mood turned sour.

Afterword

The major historical event in this story is true. Many of the characters named were real people who took part in this piece of history. Hannah and her family came from the author's imagination, in order to draw the reader into the reality of the Pemaquid colony. Smaller events in the story are those that all of us—author and readers—can only wish might have happened.

S. W-W.

Bibliography

Bickford, Kiley. "The Women and Children of Colonial Pemaquid" in *Friends of Colonial Pemaquid Newsletters* 27 & 29. New Harbor, ME: 2010 & 2011.

Brach, H.S. *Norumbega Mawooshen and the Wawenoc Diaspora.* Davistown Museum, Liberty, ME. Pennywheel Press, Hulls Cove, ME: 2008.

Cawood, Frank W. & Associates, Inc. *The Folk Remedy Encyclopedia: Olive Oil, Vinegar, Honey and 1,001 Other Home Remedies.* FC&A Medical Publishing, Peachtree City, GA: 2004.

De Paoli, Neill, Project Director. "Guns, Politics, and Furs," An Archeological and Historic Exhibit at Fort William Restoration, Colonial Pemaquid State Historic Site, Pemaquid, ME: 2008.

————. *Life on the Edge: Community and Trade on the Anglo-American Periphery, Pemaquid, Maine 1610-1689.* Ph.D. dissertation, University New Hampshire: May 2001.

————. "Recreation of Dwellings of the 1600s Begins at Colonial Pemaquid" in *The Free Press:* June 24, 2010.

————. "Pemaquid and the Defense of the Eastern Frontier, 1677-1761. Anglo-Indian Relations." Early Pemaquid colonial history lecture. August 25, 2008.

Egger-Bovet, Howard, and Marlene Smith-Baranzeni. *Book of the American Colonies. Brown Paper School, U.S. Kids History.* Little Brown & Co., Boston: 1996.

Gage, Bob and Peggy, et al. "The Seventeenth Century Herb Garden at Colonial Pemaquid," Seminar #3, Friends of Colonial Pemaquid, New Harbor, ME: 1997.

————. "Wabanaki Days." in *Friends of Colonial Pemaquid Newsletter*

#22. New Harbor, ME: 1997

Hamilton, Ken, historian. "Culture, Customs, and History, Indigenous New England." Speech presented at Center for New England Culture, Corinth, ME: August 2008.

Hardy, Kerry. *Notes on a Lost Flute.* Down East Books, Camden, ME: 2009.

Johnston, John. *History of Bristol and Bremen.* Joel Munsell Publishing, Albany, NY: 1873

Kalman, Bobbie and Ellen Brown. *The Colonial Cook.* Crabtree Publishing Company, New York: 2002.

Kurlansky, Mark. *Cod.* Penquin Putnam, Inc., New York: 1998.

Maine Archaeological and Historical Research Institute. *The Ship Angel Gabriel 1617-1635 and Today.* Bristol, ME: 1978.

McLane, Charles B. *Islands of the Mid-Maine Coast, Vol. IV, Pemaquid Point to the Kennebec River.* The Island Institute, Rockland, Me: 1994.

Quimby, Beth. "Elderberry Business Blossoms" in *Maine Sunday Telegram:* February 7, 2010.

Roberts, Paula. "Damariscove: an Island Rich in History and Natural Treasure" in *The Lincoln County News:*August 20, 1998.

Savelle, Max, and Robert Middlekauff. Robert. *A History of Colonial America* (revised).Holt, Rinehart & Winston, Inc., NY: 1966.

Smithyman, Kathryn, and Bobbie Kalman. *Native American Food and Recipes:* "Preserving and Storing Foods", p. 25. Crabtree Publishing Co., NY: 2006.

Tierney, Tom. *Colonial and Early American Fashions.* Dover Publications, Inc., Mineola, NY: 1999.

Waldman, Carl. *Encyclopedia of Native American Tribes,* 3rd Ed. Checkmark Books, NY: 2006.

Walker, Niki, and Bobbie Kalman. *Native North American Wisdom and Gifts:* "Natural Medicines" p. 21, and "Bathing and Hygiene," p. 21. Crabtree Publishing Co., NY: 2006.

Wilson, Nancy. "Lover of Monhegan Gives Comprehensive View" in *The Lincoln County News: June 27, 2002.*

Websites:

www.atsga.org: Abenaki History

www.famousamericans.net: Madockawando

www.wikipedia.org: Madockawando and Jean Vincent d'Abbadie de St. Castin